TURN TO THE BACK FOR A HELPFUL NAVIGATION GUIDE FOR PARENTS

More support materials available on our website flyingstartbooks.com/parents

Max Monkey
and Other Stories

A Red Rocket Readers Collection

Contents

TURN TO THE BACK FOR A HELPFUL NAVIGATION GUIDE FOR PARENTS

More support materials available on our website flyingstartbooks.com/parents

Collected edition first published in 2018 by Red Rocket Readers, an imprint of Flying Start Books Ltd.
Individual tltles first published in 2004 by Red Rocket Readers, an imprint of Flying Start Books Ltd.
13/45 Karepiro Drive, Auckland 0932, New Zealand.

Max Monkey. © Pam Holden, Illustrations © Jacqueline East
A Quick Picnic. © Pam Holden, Illustrations © Christine Ross
Are You Hungry? Story © Pam Holden, Illustrations © Kelvin Hawley
My Hands. Story © Pam Holden, Illustrations © Kelvin Hawley
Show Me a Shape. Story © Pam Holden, Illustrations © Jenny Cooper
Spots and Stripes. Story © Pam Holden, Illustrations © Pauline Whimp
The Flying Monkey. Story © Pam Holden, Illustrations © Jacqueline East
Watch Me Swim. Story © Pam Holden, Illustrations © Christine Hansen
ISBN 978-1-77654-198-0
Printed in India

Max Monkey

written by Pam Holden
illustrated by Jacqueline East

3

He is climbing
up in his tree.

5

He is sitting
up in his tree.

Look at the monkey!

He is scratching up in his tree.

8

He is swinging
up in his tree.

He is hiding
up in his tree.

He is coming down
from his tree.

He is going back
up his tree.

He is eating bananas
up in his tree.

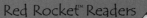

A Quick Picnic

written by Pam Holden
illustrated by Christine Ross

19

Here is the sun. That's good.

21

Here is the blanket. That's good.

Here is the umbrella.
That's good.

Here is the basket.
That's good.

Here is the food.
That's good.

29

Here is the drink.
That's good.

Here is the rain.

That's bad!

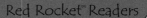

Are You Hungry?

written by Pam Holden
illustrated by Kelvin Hawley

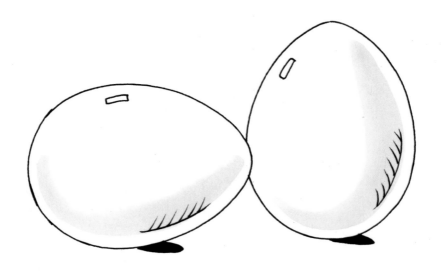

You get eggs
from the hens.

You get honey
from the bees.

39

You get apples
from the trees.

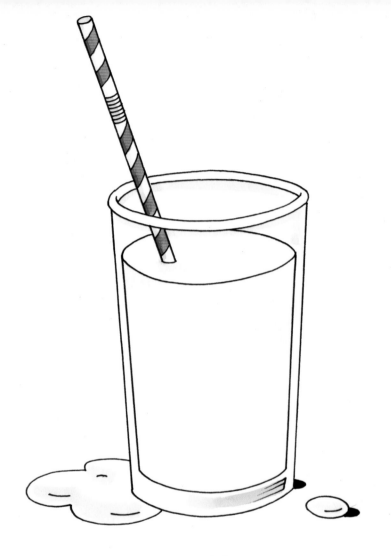

You get milk
from the cows.

You get juice
from the fruit.

You get fish
from the sea.

47

You get strawberries
from the garden.

49

You get ice-cream
from the shop!

My Hands

written by Pam Holden
illustrated by Kelvin Hawley

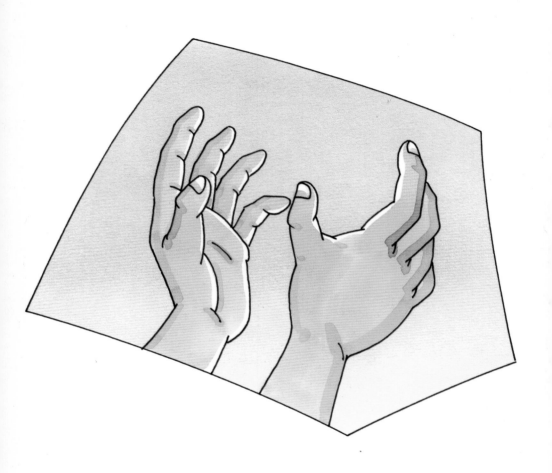

My hands are good
for lifting.

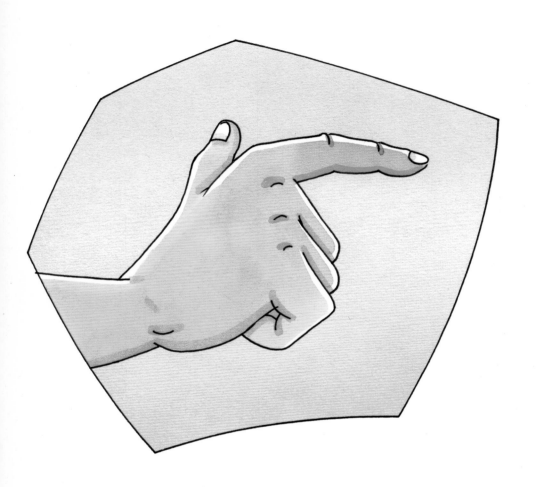

My hands are good
for touching.

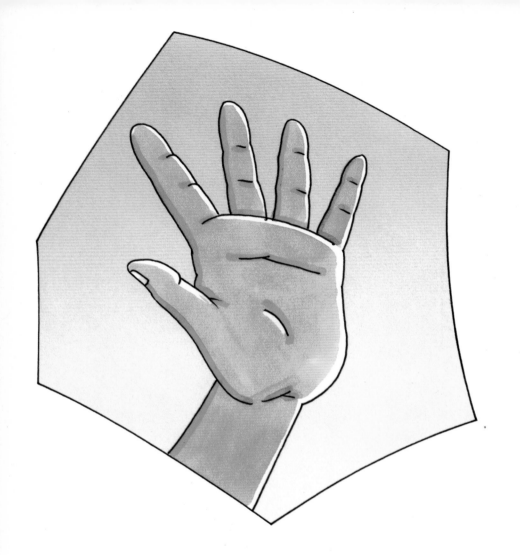

My hands are good
for waving.

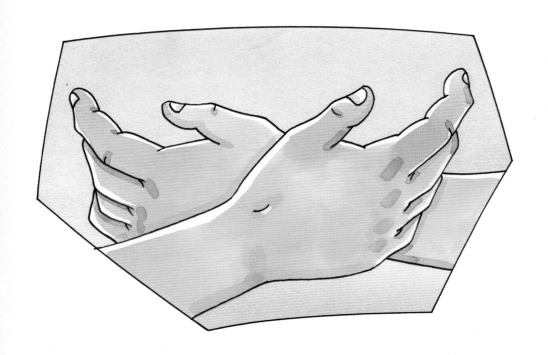

My hands are good
for holding.

My hands are good
for drawing.

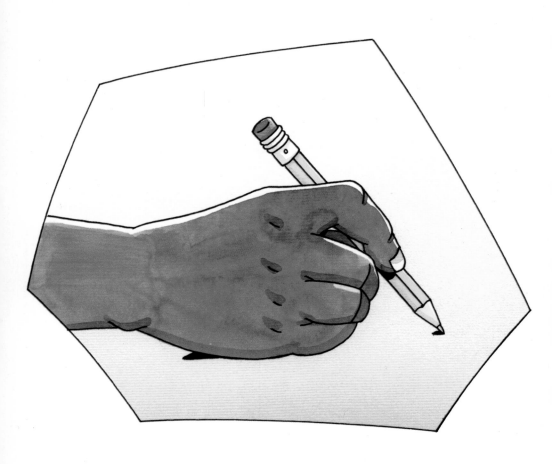

My hands are good
for writing.

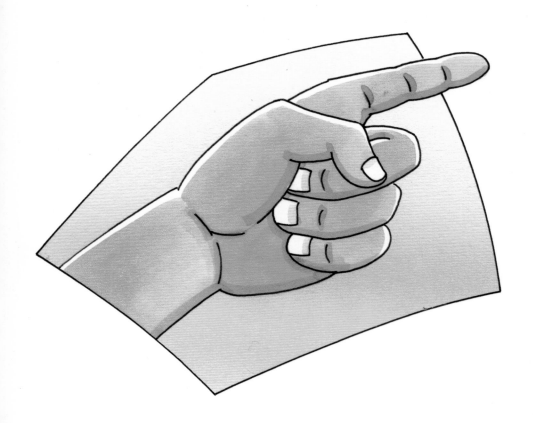

My hands are good
for pointing.

My hands are good
for clapping.

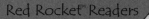

Show Me a Shape

written by Pam Holden
illustrated by Jenny Cooper

67

Show me the shape
of a ship.

Show me the shape
of a shoe.

Show me the shape
of a shirt.

73

Show me the shape
of a shark.

Show me the shape
of a shadow.

Show me the shape
of a shell.

Show me the shape
of a sheep.

Shoo! Shoo! Shoo!

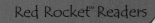

Spots and Stripes

written by Pam Holden
illustrated by Pauline Whimp

"Look! I have spots," said the giraffe.

"Look!
I have stripes,"
said the tiger.

"We have stripes,
too," said the bees.

"Look! We have
spots, too,"
said the butterflies.

91

"Look! We have
stripes, too,"
said the zebras.

"We have spots, too,"
said the ladybugs.

"Look! We have
spots **and** stripes,"
said the snakes.

"We have spots **and** stripes, too!
SSSSSSSssssssss!"

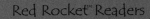

The Flying Monkey

written by Pam Holden
illustrated by Jacqueline East

My balloon went up
over the houses.

My balloon went up
over the farms.

My balloon went up
over the trees.

My balloon went up
over the hills.

My balloon went up
over the mountains.

My balloon went up
over the clouds.

My balloon went up
over the rainbow.

My balloon went
down, down,
down!

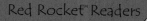

Watch Me Swim

written by Pam Holden
illustrated by Christine Hansen

"I can swim fast," said the frog.

"I can swim fast,"
said the turtle.

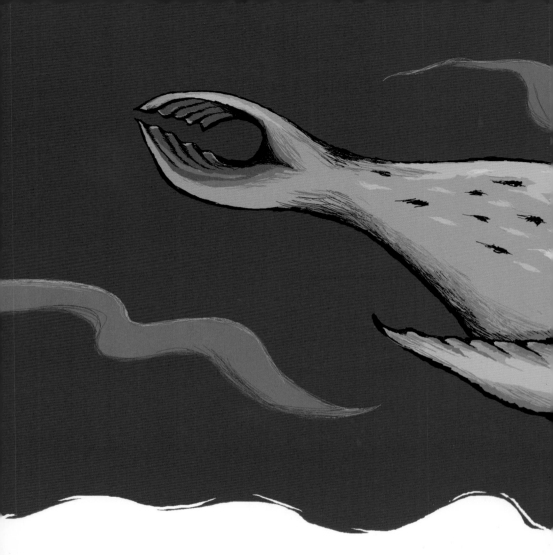

"I can swim fast," said the seal.

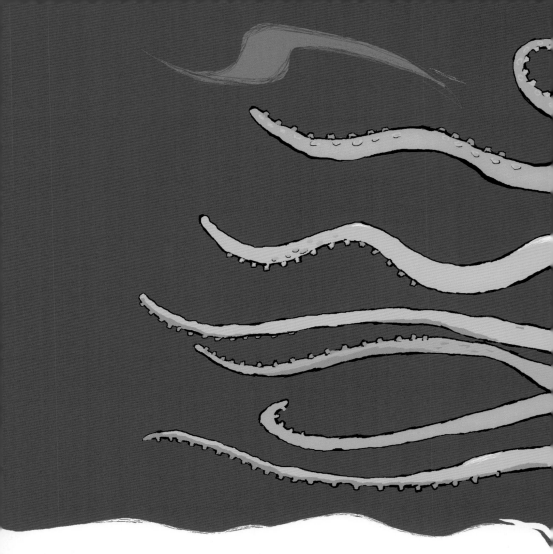

"I can swim fast," said the octopus.

"I can swim fast," said the whale.

"I can swim fast," said the shark.

"I can swim fast," said the fish.

"I can swim fast too," said the penguin.

NAVIGATION GUIDE FOR PARENTS

Support and enhance the work your child is doing at school with additional practice at every level.

Follow these steps to get them off to a flying start with literacy and learning:

1. **Picture walk and talk before you read** to introduce each story, its title and what it is about. Take a page-by-page picture walk to introduce new concepts and talk about what might happen in the story.

2. **Read together every day.** Red Rocket Readers Collections are ideal for a week of home reading practice, reading one story each day.

3. **Choose the right books!** A funny story, an interesting topic, and the right reading level – children need books that they can manage successfully and enjoy.

4. **Be positive!** It's essential that early learning-to-read experiences are positive, so praise all efforts.

These vital steps will set children up for early success!

Read more at flyingstartbooks.com/parents

INTRODUCING THE STORIES IN THIS COLLECTION

"This story is called **Max Monkey.** It's about some children who are having a picnic at the zoo. Naughty Max Monkey is looking at their picnic food. He is hungry. Read to see what he does."

Sight words: **down   from   going   He   his   in   is   up**

"This story is called **A Quick Picnic.** It's about having a lovely picnic. Have you had a picnic? What things do you need for a picnic? The people in this family have everything that they need for a good picnic. Read about what happens at their picnic."

Sight words: **good   Here   is   the**

"This story is called **Are You Hungry?** It's about lots of different foods that people love to eat. Do you like delicious food? Yum! What is your favorite food? Do you know where our food comes from?"

Sight words: **from   get   the   You**

"This story is called **My Hands.** It's about your hands and how you can do clever things with your hands. Look at your hands. Your hands are good for doing lots of things. What can you do with your hands?"

Sight words: **are   for   good   My**

"This story is called **Show Me a Shape.** It's about two tricky letters – s and h. S and h together make a new sound. It is different from s for snake and h for hat. S and h together make Sh. Can you say the sound?   Sh, Sh, Sh."

Sight words: **a   me   of   the**

"This story is called **Spots and Stripes.** It's about animals who have spots or stripes. Do you know some animals that have spots? Which animals have stripes? Where do they live? What colors are they?"

Sight words: **and   have   Look   said   the   too   we**

"This story is called **The Flying Monkey.** It's about a monkey who went for a ride in a hot-air balloon. Have you ever seen a hot-air balloon? Hot-air balloons can go up very high. It went up very high and something funny happened."

Sight words: **down   My   over   the   up   went**

"This story is called **Watch Me Swim.** It's about animals who can swim. Can you swim? Lots of animals can swim too. All the animals in this book are good swimmers. They can swim fast."

Sight words: **can   I   said   the   too**

Look For Other Titles Available Now:

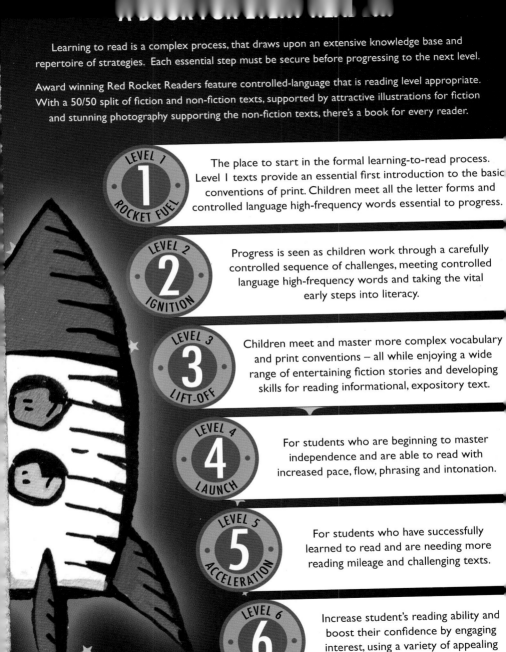

Learning to read is a complex process, that draws upon an extensive knowledge base and repertoire of strategies. Each essential step must be secure before progressing to the next level.

Award winning Red Rocket Readers feature controlled-language that is reading level appropriate. With a 50/50 split of fiction and non-fiction texts, supported by attractive illustrations for fiction and stunning photography supporting the non-fiction texts, there's a book for every reader.

LEVEL 1
1
ROCKET FUEL

The place to start in the formal learning-to-read process. Level 1 texts provide an essential first introduction to the basic conventions of print. Children meet all the letter forms and controlled language high-frequency words essential to progress.

LEVEL 2
2
IGNITION

Progress is seen as children work through a carefully controlled sequence of challenges, meeting controlled language high-frequency words and taking the vital early steps into literacy.

LEVEL 3
3
LIFT-OFF

Children meet and master more complex vocabulary and print conventions – all while enjoying a wide range of entertaining fiction stories and developing skills for reading informational, expository text.

LEVEL 4
4
LAUNCH

For students who are beginning to master independence and are able to read with increased pace, flow, phrasing and intonation.

LEVEL 5
5
ACCELERATION

For students who have successfully learned to read and are needing more reading mileage and challenging texts.

LEVEL 6
6
BOOST

Increase student's reading ability and boost their confidence by engaging interest, using a variety of appealing text types and genres.

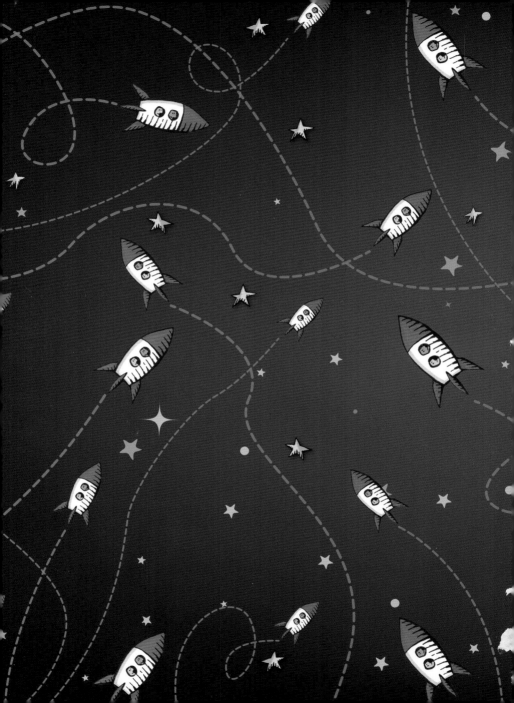